Dragonflies of Summer

Introduction

I have promised myself that I will take a break with the publishing of 'Bees' by Diana Gabaldon and also the release of series 6.

I will then adopt a policy of watching the series and reading the book and then if I still feel the inspiration writing some more light-hearted, poetic wanderings through the book and the series.

I started writing at the beginning of the Covid 19 lockdown in Wales in March 2020. I had begun watching the Outlander series at around the same time.

Since my retirement as a Police Officer in 2013, I have been volunteering several times a week with the two groups of Riding for the Disabled which operate in my local area. During lockdown it was necessary for them to cease operation.

Our Patron Princess Anne the Princess Royal made an appeal for fund raising.

I began by publishing a book of Horse and Covid Lockdown related poems any revenue generated to be donated to RDA.

Then I posted a very tongue in cheek poem on the Outlander Series Books and TV site. A number of readers asked if I had written anymore similar works.

After I had written and posted a few more – readers asked whether I had published them.

So here I am with due deference to Diana Gabaldon seven books later.

In the meantime, Season Six has been filmed and wrapped. Diana has given a publishing date for book 9 'Go Tell the Bees that I am Gone'.

The Summer is back, and the dragonflies are in the garden.

This is a book written by a fan of the Outlander Books and the TV series, for fans – it is not an Official Outlander Publication, though I do publish with the goodwill of Diana's agents.

I try not to deviate from the original plot lines and to put a poetic twist on the story and sometimes see a situation from another viewpoint.

The cover is a photograph taken by a friend and former colleague of mine Mr Leighton Benetta. I am always on the lookout for cover worthy art.

There are seventy new poems in this volume, and I have included half a dozen previously published ones which gave the book a better flow.

As readers of the Facebook sites where I post these poems may have noticed, some of my work has now drifted into the realms of the potential fantasies of the author and readers regarding Outlander and the problems that it may cause in day-to-day life. These are written with what poses as my sense of humour.

As always, I tip my hat to the phenomenon that is Diana Gabaldon, and to the cast and crew of Outlander for the quality of their work.

If anyone from that direction should ever read my work – I am open to offers!!

Readers, you seem to have enjoyed my last efforts, I hope you will enjoy this one.

All revenue raised from my work is donated to the Riding for the Disabled Charity.

Contents

It isn't

It isn't always perfect,
Awash with hearts and flowers,
Big romantic gestures,
Stars and meteor showers.

It isn't always obvious,
It creeps up unannounced,
An ambush on your senses,
You blinked and then it pounced.

It isn't always easy,
To understand the why,
You only know it happened,
A bolt out of the sky.

Two lives bound together
One heart, one mind, one soul,
One bone, one blood one body,
Two halves that make a whole.

Tempered on life's anvil
Tested by life's miles,
Weathered by life's seasons,
It will see you through life's trials

Honest, truthful, trusting,
It has no time for lies,
It knows the harm deceit can do,
The pain behind the eyes

And looking at each other,
Read the other's mind,
Second guess each other's thoughts,
Don't believe it's blind.

It just ignores life's wrinkles,
Sees you through the dark,
Cuts you deep into your soul
Indelible its mark,

And growing old together,
See, with youthful eyes,
Each knowing well the other
Not hiding in disguise.

What is this all-surrounding thing?
That grabs us from above,
Wraps us in embracing arms
Yes - you've guessed - it's love.

~

Domestic Update

Here's a little update
On the course of my affliction.
I wake up thinking Gaelic
And talk in Scottish diction!

I tried to swap the duvet
For some sheepskins and a quilt.
And keep a blade under the mattress
Where I can reach the hilt.

My hubby looks like Dougal
He's bald and wears a beard.
But his humour is like Rupert,
This makes life pretty weird.

I know he's planning something
I can read his heid.
He's scouring the free ads.
For a coat of red.

He's learned to fire a musket
The lessons were quite odd
He doesn't quite know what to do
With that great ramrod.

He talks a lot, of powder
And a lot, of balls!
There's a five-foot Brown Bess musket,
Propped up in my hall

We've had a lot of rain in Wales,
The garden is quite sodden.
Has he asked some friends around,
To re-enact, Culloden?

~

The lads Night Out

It was my ghostly birthday,
Beltane here again
Gone down the town for a few drams,
Wi the lads ye ken.

The boys had left me on my own,
Off in search of lassies,
I thought I'd get a wee kebab
And then go for a taxi.

I hauled up by the monument,
I needed a wee rest,
And saw her in a window,
Combing out a nest.

My heid was a confusion,
I did'na feel sae clever,
But that lassie in the window,
Was mine, I knew for ever.

Who is this boring looking man?
He's seen me I'm a fearing,
I'm just admiring a good view
Why is he interfering.

Ach! there are nae taxis
I must get home of course,
It's a long old way to Leoch,
Best I steal a horse!

~

Falling through Time

The flowers were, forget me nots
I knelt to pick a few,
To add to my collection,
Their pretty shade of blue.

A clump of hardy flowers,
Nestled at its base,
The massive granite standing stone,
Inches from my face,

A humming noise, A sound like screams
The crashing guns of battle
The feel of a magnetic pull,
My senses start to rattle,

I can't resist the fatal pull,
The largest stone of all,
Tempts me now to touch it,
I must obey its call.

I place my hand upon it,
The world at once is black,
The acrid smell of ozone
My senses start to crack,

I feel like I am torn apart,
Almost vaporised,
My body disassembled,
Then rematerialized.

It's a feeling like no other,
Like dropping in a lift
A crazy rollercoaster,
Or falling off a cliff,

The light is truly blinding,
Fit to mesmerise,
A hundred thousand lightbulbs
All shining in your eyes,

You hear the noises of creation
And the screaming of the dead,
A hundred new sensations
Exploding in your head,

And all this happens in a flash,
It's chaos without limit
Falling through the veil of time,
Only takes a minute.

~

Humerus Manipulation

Ye'll have tae force that shoulder back!
He can nae ride a horse
One stood behind to hold him still,
To mend his arm by force!

The lad was whiter a sheet
Sat quiet by the fire,
Stoically he nursed his wounds,
Pain making him perspire.

Stop! Don't it that way,
My nurses brain kicked in,
Could see the muscles tearing,
As the bone ripped through his skin.

You will not force the joint back,
You'll likely break his arm,
You'll cripple him if you try it,
I'll not let you do that harm.

Their leader quietly nodded,
I stepped into the fray,
I'd never seen such muscle,
On a shoulder to this day.

I looked the patient in the eye,
This next bit is the worst,
Flex the arm, raise, and rotate,
I thought his face would burst,

The final push took all my strength,
The satisfying crack!
As humerus fell into place,
The joint had been put back.

His eyes held mine, they cleared of pain,
Blue eyed boy for sure,
The look we held was not just thanks,
It screamed of something more.

I am a nurse, his lowered gaze,
He's staring at my breast
Not a wet nurse – idiot.
This is no time for jest.

Is clean not in their language?
They do not disinfect,
Well, some of them are hardly washed,
So, what can I expect?

Orders barked – I have a belt,
I'll use that for a sling,
Swab the wound with alcohol,
That should make it sting.

It seems I am recruited,
The leader sees my worth,
They do not have a healer,
Well not this side of Perth!

I travel with the patient,
Remember – you're a wife!
I could not tell this was the day
I'd start a brand-new life!

~

Second time Around

It was a formal document
Writ with quill and ink
Sat on a log I read it.
And took down a stiff drink.

But I already had a husband
Though he was not yet born
How could I take another one?
Tomorrow in the morn.

The groom did not seem worried
In fact, he seemed quite sure.
It didn't seem to faze him.
That I'd done it all before.

I stamped my feet a little.
And had another drink.
I think I drank the bottle
While I had a think.

It wasn't really bigamy
Frank was not yet due
Was Jamie then my first husband.
Had he just jumped the queue!

I did get very drunk that day
I don't remember night
I woke up with a steaming head.
And looking quite a fright.

But someone had produced a dress
And a very charming ring.
A church bedecked with candles
And a priest to do his thing.

And oh, my when I saw the groom
Dressed in highland splendour.
I had a feeling that the wedding night
Would see my heart surrender.

~

The Wedding Night

There was a certain atmosphere
In the room above the Inn,
The all-male wedding party
Were, making quite a din,

Despite the lack of planning,
There was really, quite a spread
The wine and whisky flowing,
Washing down the meat and bread.

This wasn't my first wedding night,
But the last was much more quiet,
Without the punctuation,
Of Clansmen fit to riot,

I'd shed the dress, kicked off my shoes,
And sat there in my stays
Combing out my pinned-up hair,
Planning what to say.

Dougal wanted witnesses,
To be sure we didn't cheat.
Would Rupert and – hell -Angus
Want a front row seat!

My thoughts were interrupted,
I pulled out of my gloom,
The door was softly opened,
To admit – the groom.

We talked and drank into the night,
I asked a lot of questions,
We learned of each other's families.
Discussed and made suggestions.

And when we finally got to bed,
To make it all official,
The depth of his emotion
Was far from superficial.

Suffice to say my virgin groom
Proved to be quite a scholar
And by the time the sun came up
He'd learned how to make me holler!

The Wedding night – re visited

Atmosphere electric
With sparks that lit the gloom,
An illuminated elephant
occupied the room!

Awkward, empty silence,
I contemplate my fate,
Am I cheating on my husband?
I must leave, but it's too late.

His wedding night, a virgin,
No time for romance,
Married off to save my skin,
A match of circumstance.

We drink, we talk, he entertains,
The atmosphere crackles,
Who will take that leap of faith?
And break these moral shackles.

I pray she can'nae read me,
My bits are all unlinking,
Ungodly thoughts run through my head
it's not my mind that's thinking

To bed? I'll help ye with yer stays
My fingers are all thumbs,
I touch her skin, like ivory,
Her beauty strikes me dumb,

Her hands are reaching for my belt,
Her turn, she takes command,
I hear it drop, my senses hop,
Into a foreign land.

I've waited for this kiss so long,
Her lips are soft and yielding
Please God don't break this magic,
I must control these feelings,

Our bodies join, all reason lost,
She grips me like a vice
Her arms and legs wrap round me,
To hell with all advice.

It never was like this with Frank,
It feels like a betrayal,
This is a joining of two souls,
And he's definitely all male!

Nocturnal exploration,
Two bodies become one,
I made him call out for his God,
Before the night was done.

In candlelight I watch him sleep,
Sweet smile upon his face,
A body forged of iron,
Is this man now my place?

Watch and learn she told me,
Feel your way around,
I know just what she's liking,
For she makes a squeaky sound,

She thinks that I am sleeping,
But I'm planning in my head,
The things that I might do tae her,
When my wife comes back tae bed!

Under Surveillance

Dougal said tae follow her,
Report on what she did,
She a canny one and slippery,
Keeps her motives hid,

We can'nae stop to take a breath,
She's always on the move,
Picking herbs or healing folk,
What is she trying to prove?

Now me and my wee Angus,
In the kitchen like to hide
We just get settled in the snug,
She's waiting there outside,

Carry this, fetch me that,
Take this out and bring that in,
A female sergeant Major,
Sure, she's makin' ma heid spin.

Young Jamie's got the hots for her,
He's putty in her hands,
He'll nae think any bad of her,
That red haired firebrand

She's trouble walking on two legs,
She does'nae know her place,
cursing that would shame a saint,
Comes from that pretty face.

She's classy – kind 'a grows on you,
Has a witty sense of humour,
I think I heard her make a joke,
Or was that just a rumour,

Then she and Jamie married,
I think he met his match,
If she can keep that man alive,
She's really, quite a catch.

Now we have stopped watching,
But she still will not obey,
Ye can'nae leave her anywhere,
In one place, she'll not stay.

Rescued from the Captains hands,
The Laird expects a scandal,
Will he have to pacify?
An irate Blackjack Randall?

Jamie, discipline yer wife,
Do not spare the strap,
I'll nae get killed because of her,
Make sure she shuts her trap.

~

Going to a Barbecue!

A stranger in a stranger land,
I found my niche in life,
Herbalist and charmer,
And the procurators wife.

And yes, I have been other things,
As I came through the years,
Witch may well be one of them,
I pray on people's fears.

I'm here tae fight for Scotland,
For freedom from the lies,
To put the prince upon his throne,
The end of British ties.

Why are you here? Why did ye come?
All travellers have a reason,
Ye say it was an accident,
Yet yer involved in treason!

Be careful Claire, I warn ye,
These simple folks all itch,
They'll turn on ye, in seconds.
Burn ye for a witch!

I know the powers of darkness,
They help me in my cause,
I'll get my way, through magic,
Healing is your course!

Ye are here for a reason,
Ye may not know it yet,
Yer braw fox cub, he loves ye
He'll get here, I will bet!

My Dougal, he will find a way,
He will rescue me!
They can'nae burn an innocent!
And I'm with child ye see,

That canny lawyer plays for time,
He surely knows his art,
He knows he can'nae save us both,
We're condemned from the start!

We both bear the devils mark,
The townsfolk think it so,
We are the entertainment!
We are the greatest show!

When we hear the verdict Claire
I'll be wearing not a stitch,
The pagan folk of Cranesmuir,
Will nae barbecue this witch!

~

Jamie Gives a Lesson

Auld Alex called him to his work,
Our tryst would have to wait,
I'd meet him in the hayloft,
We made ourselves a date,

Warm above the horses,
Snug amongst the hay,
Newly married privacy,
We came up here to play!

Sound of footsteps down below,
There is no place to hide.
Young Hamish looking for a horse,
Wild Donas he would ride.

Boastful youth, his pride was hurt
He'd fallen from his horse,
A better mount was needed,
He was not scared of course.

Half broken Sorrel Stallion
This would restore his pride,
  Just the sort of animal,
Son of the Laird would ride.

Swift down from the hayloft,
  Straight and to the point,
  Hamish needs a lesson,
  His nose is out of joint.

  I listen to them talking,
    From the loft above,
  Having talked of horses,
  Hamish turned to love.

  Sleeping with a woman,
  Is it nice to share a bed?
I could hear Jamie blushing,
  Through the words he said.

  He wanted to get married,
    I smelled alright ye see,
He knew from what his father said,
  The right lass – that was me.

Looking up he met my eye,
tears of laughter, stream
We're getting to the crux of this,
He's having a bad dream

John says – what John is that
Oh! John the Stable lad?
Ye do it just like horses?
I can hear him blushing bad,

Between two ripe tomatoes,
The matter was explained,
Hamish doubtful of the facts,
Jamie's voice more pained.

I'd near bitten through my finger,
Stifling my mirth,
Thank goodness that the lecture
Was not on giving birth!

Passed down by a cousin,
With some skill in the acts
The future Laird of Leoch,
Learned some useful facts!

Broken

First, he broke resistance down
Pain his favourite tool,
He used it like a master,
Subtlety so cruel,

He made me scream, he made me beg,
He made my want to cry,
He took the very heart of me,
He made me want to die.

He took my inner being,
Destroyed my sense of self,
The lowest things he made me do
Just tools upon his shelf,

Then he took my mind apart
Made me think of you,
Put himself there, in my thoughts,
I could not split the two,

He burned, he flogged, he punished,
He raped and raped again.
Nothing but surrender
Would feed his lust for pain.

He took me as a lover would,
Demanding I respond,
Easing pain with soothing oil,
As magic from a wand.

And he became you in my mind,
Corrupted every cell
I saw him above me
But I saw you as well!

His final act destroyed my soul,
He made me find release,
Pleasure lying in his arms,
Anything for peace!

Then he made me brand myself,
A perverted work of art,
Acknowledge that he owned me,
And from you I had to part.

You cannot heal a broken man,
Whose inner shell is gone,
There is no foundation,
The pain goes on and on.

Time may smooth some parts away,
But in my darkest nights,
His memory will make me scream,
As my body fights.

Sleep will be a stranger,
He will reclaim my mind,
Come clawing back into my thoughts,
Like the memory he rewinds,

Touch me gently, be my peace,
Let me feel you there,
Call me home with loving words,
Back to this one we share,

Then hold me in the darkness,
Take me to a time before,
Make your arms my fighting strength,
you only are my cure.

Facing Demons

He lay in pain, he would not eat,
Tormented in his mind,
Body craving gentle sleep,
No respite he could find.

His hand would heal, his back would mend
His body I could fix,
The demon there inside his mind,
Was always in the mix.

Fever burned his flesh away
Nothing made him cool
Was he now fighting to die?
Had he changed the rule.

I will not let you leave me,
I'm stubborn just like you,
I prayed to God to heal your soul,
He will tell me what to do.

I conjured up a spectre,
A date with darkness kept
Through the smoke of poppies
While the Abbey slept.

His demon I confronted
A simulacrum of me,
smelled of oil of lavender,
It would not let him be.

I baited him with loving words,
I challenged him to live,
To chase the spectre from his mind,
I had no more to give,

He hunted me across the room,
His hands closed round my neck
We danced a deadly tango,
Nothing held in check.

Blue eyes blazing, fever hot
Berserk and fit to kill,
The fever broke, the madness cleared,
He buckled to my will.

We fell, entangled to the floor,
He sobbed into my breast,
Cried for everything he'd lost,
His mother and the rest,

We lay there 'til the morning,
Exhausted by the fight,
Then he asked for breakfast,
And held my body tight.

His strength would soon recover
His mind would take much more,
But I will heal this stubborn man,
My love will be his cure

~

A Hot Bath.

A cave beneath the monastery
Dark as blessed night,
A hot spring fills a pitch-black lake.
Stars provide the only light.

I floated in the darkness
Feeling myself heal
Warmth invaded all my scars
I began once more to feel

Water washed right through my soul
I felt the pain depart
Maybe it could heal us both
Of sorrows to our hearts.

I thought of all she'd said and done
Her selfless act of courage
Her desperate plea that she could heal
My mind and then our marriage.

I will bring her to this sacred place.
Hold her in my arms
Let the water do its work
Let the heat work all its charms.

We need to find connection
We need to find a path
And I know what she misses most.
Claire loves a good hot bath.

~

When Ye Were Nae Watchin!

Ye could nae see me watching,
Drawn there from afar,
Like a moth to candle flame,
To you my guiding star.

Ye could nae see me searching,
Lost in life's dark maze,
Emerging from its darkness,
I held you in my gaze.

Ye did nae ken I needed you,
As flowers need the rain,
Purgatory, endless,
You could salve the pain.

Ye would nae say ye felt the same,
Yer heart as lost as mine,
My eyes met yours and locked there,
Surely fates design.

Ye will nae leave me Sassenach,
I will nae let ye go,
Our time on earth, no time at all,
For endless love tae grow,

Ye will nae be without me,
When death throws out it's lures
My body gone, bone of my bone
My soul will join with yours.

Ye did nae see the way I watched,
From that day we met,
There could nae be another then,
There has nae been one yet.

Ye do nae need tae worry,
When all of life is gone,
I'll hold you safe wrapped in my arms,
My body keeps you warm,

Do ye not remember,
The night ye made yer mark,
Wrapped in plaid in front of me,
That long ride through the dark.

49

I will nae live without ye,
Ye know ye keep me whole,
Two halves joined by endless love,
One mind, one life, one goal.

Ye ken I'm no sae brave as then,
We've both been through some wars,
I've not the energy of youth,
To settle up old scores,

Come lie with me, I need ye,
Our bodies will enmesh
I possess ye and I worship ye,
Oh! mistress of my flesh.

~

An Enemy is Made

Jamie's with his cousin,
My word they can talk,
Their minds are on the business,
I'm going for a walk.

Sailors running everywhere,
Loading and unloading,
Ships disgorging all their goods,
They empty what they're holding.

Something wrong has caught my eye,
Sailors wrapped in shrouds,
Carried to the warehouse,
Hidden in the crowd.

My healer's instinct drives me there,
I'm drawn to interfere,
Why are they hiding bodies?
The answer is quite clear.

I pull aside the hammock shroud,
I see that flat red rash,
The pustules hiding in the mouth,
Diagnosis in a flash,

Thank God I've had the vaccine,
I cannot catch this pox
It is Le Petit Variole,
Smallpox – on the docks.

The Count would keep it hidden,
For he will lose his ship,
They'll burn it, and the cargo.
No profit then – this trip.

I have my sacred duty,
This disease must not be spread,
The word is out, the port is closed,
The Count has lost his head.

burning barrels. burning ship,
A fortune lost to fire,
And we have made an enemy,
With consequences dire!

Parisian to the core

When I was a still a child
I made a big mistake.
I stole something from a Scotsman
A little wooden snake.

Of very little value
To anyone but him.
I stole it from his sporran
And he didn't feel a thing.

It changed my life forever,
That's when I met milord.
For that is what I called him
When my future he assured.

He took me from the brothel
I was born there, no excuse
And he paid me to steal for him
My talent put to use.

He vowed he would look after me
If I lost a hand,
Or any other body part
In the service of his land.

And I am married his daughter
No longer a French rake
Maybe stealing Sawny,
Was not such a mistake.

For milord adopted me
When we married by the sea
Fergus Claudel Fraser.
I have his name and family.

~

After the Bastille

The thing I wouldn't tell him
But from my face, he knew.
He has acute perception
Of everything I do.

Laid out in terms of black and white,
A deal to save a life,
Like the one he made for me
When I was first his wife.

It wasn't that I'd done the act,
But that I didn't trust,
That he would see the reason,
I had done what I must.

A complex man, but simple
In many ways I've found,
He sees things clear as right or wrong
There is no middle ground.

Lying naked in the grass,
We talk of things unjust,
With little blocks of honesty,
We try and rebuild trust.

With mortar made of unsaid words
And grievances unaired,
Reassurance forms a roof,
Our shelter is repaired.

Then there is possession,
Can the occupants move in?
One blood, one bone, one body,
One soul, one love, one skin.

Time will never part us,
Our whole is far too brave,
But for now, we cling together,
Like two souls in a cave.

Dishonesty of Princes

No burdens now upon us,
We had returned from France,
We mourned for Faith and mended,
Enjoyed life's slow advance,

Lallybroch was home now,
The place we both loved most,
Then fate comes knocking at the door,
It brought the monthly post.

Books from France for Jenny,
Bills all for the farm
One for me from Jared
This one was only harm.

It called me loyal, and honourable
Commended me as brave,
Bid me fight hard for the prince,
The life of Scotland save.

The last thing was a parchment,
It bore the Stuart seal,
I opened it with hands that shook,
Not knowing what to feel.

The declaration written,
Stamped with the Stuart ring
Proclaimed a King of England
The Divine right of Kings.

Below a list of Chieftains,
Signed in formal hand,
Swore him their allegiance,
To help him claim the land.

The wee dishonest bastard,
I called him all things rotten,
He'd forged my signature in full
Right there at the bottom.

James Alexander Malcolm Mackenzie Fraser,
In all its formal glory,
The name once more a traitor,
Can we not escape this story?

Am faclair beag! Mac am Diabhail
I cursed him to his soul,
Can Claire and I not live at peace,
Is War the only goal.

So, it's off the raise an army,
Call the Fraser Clan
Bait the Old Fox in his den
Another cheating man.

~

Foot Rot

Men are quite disgusting,
When it comes to feet,
They hardly ever wash them,
Or keep them smelling sweet,

When I saw wee Angus
Pulling off his socks,
I saw a sight so horrible,
I near fainted with the shock.

Toenails, brown and curly,
With fungus quite obscene
The rotting skin between his toes,
Starting to go green.

He found it very funny
When I tried to explain
Why a soldier needed healthy feet,
To march to war again.

I told him he should wash his socks,
And keep them clean and dry,
Take them off in the fresh air,
Then I thought he'd cry.

His toothless smile just grinned at me,
Assured me he was fine,
The smell would scare the redcoats,
Standing smartly in a line

Then he pulled his kilt up
And nearly died of shock
The green stuff thriving on his feet,
Was growing on his cock!

~

Cannon Blast

Dogged and determined,
He staggered through the door,
Pushing past the English,
He laid Rupert on the floor.

For himself there was no thought,
His friend was wounded bad,
He sat there as I stitched the wound,
With all the skill I had.

He watched that belly rise and fall,
Afraid his friend might die,
I should have seen the warning,
When I looked into his eye,

He swore he was just tired,
Said he needed rest,
But sat and watched the rise and fall,
Of Rupert massive chest.

Blast shock is a killer,
It doesn't like to rush,
Internal bleeding chokes your lungs,
Your insides blown to mush.

There was no one to tell me
As he breathed his last,
Choked on blood come from his lungs,
About the cannon blast.

Oh faithful, ragged warrior,
You terrier of men,
Brave as one made twice your size,
We won't see your like again.

Looking straight into my eyes,
His anguish now laid bare,
His dying words in gasps of blood,
Help me mistress Claire!

~

A Deer Fly!

All around is peace and quiet,
Riding through the heather,
Murtagh with the pack horse,
Gives us distance for our leisure,

I'm warned about his Grandsire,
He of many faces,
A scheming twister of man,
Who has no saving graces!

Horses plod on steadily,
Nodding with each stride,
Content and honest in their work,
Their patience not yet tried.

Lost in conversation,
I did not see it land,
Buzzing round my horse's ears,
Evading Jamie's hand.

Flying jaws of evil
give my hero such a bite
A full-blown Gaelic highland scream,
Puts his horse to flight,

Panicked horse and rider,
The horse has gone quite mad
He's clinging on by any means,
A mass of legs and plaid.

The accompaniment of language,
Would make a sailor blush,
He climbs back in the saddle,
His face all red with flush,

Murtagh chuckles quietly,
We ride along the grass,
'Is Yon Jamie in a hurry then,
To meet his grandsire – lass?'

He falls in alongside me
Horse suitably chastened,
Thanks to one small deer fly,
Our journey has been hastened.

A horse, gun safe and battle trained,
Has overcome new fears,
Now trained for Gaelic highland yells,
Two feet behind his ears!

~

One Winner

Clan Mackenzie should be mine,
I'm brother to the Laird,
I've sired his son, I do his will,
His war chief if he cared

His twisted legs won't carry him,
He will not live too long,
Hamish is too young ye ken,
I am the one, I'm strong.

Calum has another plan,
He'd go outside the Clan,
Our nephew, our sister's boy,
Will be my brother's man.

So, I will keep Young Jamie close,
Keep him in my eye,
Who knows the course a life can take?
The reckless boy may die.

My passion is for Scotland,
A Stuart on the throne,
Jacobite runs through my heart,
In solid granite stone.

Our nephew is a canny one,
He has a way with men,
I see how people draw to him,
The follow him ye Ken.

He learned to tame his reckless streak,
The boy is now a man,
Marriage to the Sassenach,
That will aid my plan.

Then if he dies in prison,
His wife should marry me,
To keep her safe, a traitor's wife,
She'd get his land ye see.

My scheming brain works overtime,
He plays me like a game,
Gives me power but not enough,
My temper soon will flame,

Right from the beginning,
That axe wound on his head,
Determined that this thing will end,
When one of us is dead.

Jamie is a diplomat
One to surf the tide,
To keep his people safe from harm,
Not into battle ride.

I can'nae help but love him,
He is my Fraser kin,
When Calum dies, the fight is on,
And only one can win!

~

The 45

Walk quietly, revere the names,
Do not make a sound,
Listen and you'll hear the cries,
The souls beneath the ground,

The men who faced the canon,
The men who charged, the guns,
Mown down in a hail of lead,
The clansmen and their sons.

Fighting for a way of life
escape from English rule,
Men at arms, and farmers,
All led there by a fool.

Listen and you'll hear the pipes,
Skirl across the moor,
Unearthly feet will run on grass,
As they did before,

Battle cries, and bravery,
The clash of sword and dirk,
Scotland's finest blown apart,
Less than an hour's work,

Cumberland was brutal,
The day would end in slaughter,
Wounded shot, bodies burned,
The British gave no quarter,

A lifetime lying neath the moor,
Named stones above their head,
Listen and you'll hear them,
As you mourn your dead,

Place your tributes carefully,
Respect the ground below,
Those warrior souls are listening,
From their beds below.

This bare and bleak forbidding place,
Preserves a time before,
Its echo carries on the breeze,
Across Culloden Moor

The fight for freedom still goes on,
Thank God you are alive,
Minutes killed a way of life,
It took just 45.

~

I Am Not Mad!

I sit in bed and listen,
I see the shoulder shrugs
I am talked about in riddles,
Pacified with drugs.

I am not mad!
I do not want to be here,
I want to be with him,
He sent me back to keep me safe,
Not just on a whim.

I am not mad!
I need no imagination,
I know the cost of war,
The man I love intends to die,
Or he will hang for sure.

I am not mad!
I hang on to my sanity,
I'm carrying his child,
A child conceived of endless love,
I have not been defiled.

I am not mad!
Turn off the noises of this time,
Reminding me of violence
Turn them off! they hurt my mind,
Let me hear just silence.

I am not mad!
I hear you talk about me,
As if I am not here,
Discuss my body and my mind,
Have I not made it clear?

I am not mad!
You cannot understand it,
Your narrow minds will blow,
But check through history, I'm there!
200 years ago!

I am not mad!

First Steps

A new life in America,
He thought it best we go,
I had no choice, I was his wife,
What he said was so.

A child to bring up as his own,
Complete him as a man,
The father who lived in my mind
Was not part of his plan.

Boston called, his high-powered job,
I'm now professor's wife,
A bauble hanging from his arm,
Domesticated life.

Rubber lands on tarmac
Metal steps so steep,
Is this yet another world?
Please help me make the leap.

He reaches out to guide me,
I take hold of his hand,
The one I grasp is in my mind,
And this is not his land.

My feet should rest on heather,
My soul is cold as ice,
But I must stay for he is gone.
We all will pay a price.

~

A Cave with A View

Twas hell after Culloden,
I could nae live with folk,
My face on all the broadsheets
Life was nae such a joke.

High upon the hillside,
A place found as a child,
Hiding in the yellow gorse,
Where everything grows wild.

Its entrance is quite hidden,
A slit between two rocks,
Just space to slip between them,
A door which never locks.

It is a place of solitude,
Enough space just for one,
Some books, a bed upon the floor,
A fire – it could be fun!

I held my nerve for all that time,
I kept my family fed,
The redcoats did nae go away,
The King sent more instead,

He will subdue the Highlands,
Kill a way of life,
I will just be thankful
He did nae kill my wife,

I pray she's found her calling,
I hope it worked out well,
I hate Frank down to his bones,
But he loves her, I can tell.

Not passionate as I am,
He does'nae make her scream,
As I can – when I cross through time,
And hold her in my dream.

So, we took the English gold,
Their money for my life,
Prison is an ugly place
Tae dream about yer wife.

Twas only desperation,
The human will to live,
Keeping safe the ones I love,
While I had life to give.

Bravery is different,
Surviving is a knack,
Living life from hour to hour,
With eyes around yer back.

They named me the Dun Bonnet,
For the hat I came to wear,
They'd know Red Jamie Fraser,
By the colour of his hair.

I've been told that people come,
They pay to see my cave,
They look in through the entrance,
Remark that I was brave.

Occupied for seven years,
Ian showed my daughter,
One bedroom cave, with stunning views,
With damp and running water.

Punishment posting

Grey Stone, Grey sky, and Major Grey,
Sent here in disgrace,
A hell hole of a prison
Miles from societies grace,

Here they hold the Jacobites,
All traitors to the Crown,
Resentful starving, dirty,
In shades of grey and brown.

Honour says I make the best,
It's a punishment of posting,
Best write home to mother now,
From her I'll get a roasting,

My quarters are quite comfortable,
Apart from rats and mice,
Distant from the prisoners,
Rank with fleas and lice.

Quarrie, says the hunting's fair,
But all is damp and cold,
And don't waste time on looking,
For the French Kings gold.

And one Jacobite prisoner,
Still chained amongst the men
Big Red Jamie Fraser,
You know his reputation then?

He's spokesman for the prisoners,
You need him on your side,
They will do nought without his say,
From stubbornness and pride.

He's highly educated,
Well-read I must confess,
I dine with him once every week,
He likes a game of chess.

Yes, I know Red Jamie,
I saw him in the yard,
Watchful eyes, surveying me
I think he's marked my card.

Will he recognise the boy?
Who tried to take his life!
Then told him of the army's plans,
Lest he rape his wife!

They brought him chained into the room,
Pleasantries exchanged,
Deep blue eyes looked down at me,
As if I were deranged.

Then he spoke, his highland voice
Had me quite unnerved!
What did ye do tae be sent here,
I hope it was deserved!

~

Lust

He sat out in the prison yard,
His noble features proud,
Eyes burning, ever watchful,
Attentive in the crowd,

All hearing and all seeing,
noting my arrival,
A change of Governor will impact,
On prisoner survival.

The only man the jailers fear,
The only man in chains,
He is the very devil
Colonel Quarry now explains.

He is a man of learning,
The man commands respect,
He speaks for the prisoners,
Their spokesman elect!

The name Red Jamie Fraser,
Ripples down my spine,
He and I have history,
He is no friend of mine.

He shrugs down in his blanket,
Talks quietly to his men,
Walks quietly back into the cell,
The fox is in his den.

In time I grow to like him,
He is erudite, urbane,
Like me he lost someone he loves,
I can feel his pain.

I'll not send him over oceans
I shall keep him close by me,
Something deep inside my heart,
Won't let me set him free.

My mind covets his body,
That part I can't possess,
I will settle for his friendship,
a thing words cannot express.

I must leave!

Before it's obvious,
I can see it now,
My bones, my eyes, my attitude,
He looks like me – and how!

I must leave!

Leave while there is still a chance,
For he is mine – no doubt!
A pardon writ, I'm going home,
Before the truth gets out

I am going!

When the truth sank in,
It truly broke his heart,
The tantrum rocked the stable yard,
I'd torn his world apart.

I am going!

I am a stinking papist,
He would be one like me,
I baptised him William James
He has my rosary.

He left!

I cried and watched him ride away,
Never looking back,
I called the man I'd loved since birth,
He rode off down the track,

I ran

I tried my best to follow,
But others held me tight,
I screamed, I cried, I tried to run,
I fought with all my might.

Don't go

So tall, so strong, and quiet and kind
My comfort as a child,
He taught me everything I know,
He stopped me running wild

Forever

If our paths should meet again,
I will not forget,
Son of mine – ye have my heart,
You do not know it yet!

Blood

Our lives are two sides of a coin,
You are heads, and I am tails,
Joined together by our blood,
Which binds when all else fails.

Goodbye

I said goodbye and rode away,
For this was not my place,
Could not look back lest ye should see
The tears run down my face.

~

A lost Soul

Going through the motions,
For all those missing years,
Decisions made without a thought
For other people's fears.

Lacking in emotion,
Not caring if I died,
Survival shows the worst in men
I've cheated and I've lied.

Ye see my finger tapping,
Ye ken all of my tells,
You know just what I'm thinking,
Tis one of yer spells.

Decisions that I would ha made,
Are harder now with you,
I've not just me tae think of,
It's a consequence for two.

Like spring has come into my life,
Returning to dead ground,
Feelings lost in years of frost,
Are waiting to be found.

Green leaves of hope are sprouting,
Flowers of joy will bloom,
That light that shines into my heart,
When you light up my room.

Yesterday I'd nothing
Except to carry on,
Today I've a whole life to live,
Tis you that brought the sun.

Joy and hope, oh yes and fear,
Rush in and I must choose,
Yesterday I'd nothing
Now I've so much more tae lose.

Smugglers Moon

Smuggling is an art form,
To do it well ye find,
Planning aye and cunning,
A certain state of mind.

Bribery, corruption,
Grease the right man's palm,
Put trust in the wrong one,
You may well come to harm.

A boat was due from Jared,
Goods coming from France
Unloaded on an Arbroath beach
Lead customs men a dance.

They were waiting for us,
Hiding out in force
Chaos on the cliff top,
It couldn't be much worse,

Run lads, each man for himself,
Jamie shouted loud,
Red hair gleaming in the night,
He stood out in the crowd.

I would find out later,
Who hanged the customs man?
A complicated, devious plot,
It was part of their plan.

Men were running everywhere,
No one knew their way,
One grabbed me hand over my mouth,
I would not die today.

Confusion, chaos all around,
I could not heed their calls,
I bit the hand which held my mouth,
And kicked Fergus in the balls!

~

The Morning After

Was I ashamed, ashamed of what?
I sat high on the hill
Ashamed to bring my true wife home
Think of me what ye will

Anger burned so fiercely
And she would slip away
I had to try and stop her
Don't let her leave I pray

I watched my sister let her go,
Send her from my home
What does Jenny want from me?
She knows I'm made to roam

Too late I reached the door yard,
Claire was gone for good
And Jenny packed a bag for her
A week's supply of food.

I raged, I cursed, I shouted
I called my sister bad
We both threw things, we trashed the house,
The thought just drove me mad.

I must ride and catch her
But I've Laoghaire back to beg,
Wailing like a banshee
Hanging on my leg.

This stops now- she has to go
I really din'nae care,
She knows I cannot love her,
My love is all for Claire.

I tried tae tell her gently,
To calm down her alarm
But she took my pistol
She shot me through the arm.

Let me die of fever,
Though for her hands I yearn,
I don't want her to pity me,
Then leave and not return

I felt Claire coming back to me
In my fevered mind,
Tending me and caring
Gentle hands and kind.

In sweat-soaked dreams, the truth would out,
My love I would declare,
And all the time she had come back
I cannot lie to Claire.

Bare my arse! what spell is this,
My senses on alarm
A needle stabbed into my bum
How will this cure my arm.

Germs ye say – wee beasties
This is witchcraft now, I know,
I'm sure I should a let ye burn,
All those years ago

~

Joan's Thoughts

She brought a Da into our lives,
He loved us as his own,
Promised to look after us,
Until we were full grown,

But Ma has troubles in her mind,
She can'nae see her way,
Her weeping and her wailing
Will not make him stay.

Her mind is dwelling in the past,
And she cannot forgive,
When he went with that Sassenach,
That Witch should never live.

And now she's married half the man,
For Da is always sad,
He loves us dear but longs for her,
And the life that he once had.

He cannot make her happy,
Jealousy consumes,
That Witch she sees is always there,
Hiding in the room.

She will use his name and status,
She'll make him send her gold,
She says he's hers and she won't part,
Until her grave be cold.

In truth, he tried, it couldn't work,
For he was never free,
They meet each other through all time,
The English Witch and he.

I've ne'er seen Ma so angry,
The Witch back from the dead,
Ma was called to Lallybroch
And found them both in bed.

Ma could not fight the love they have,
Not with an ill wish charm,
Deranged and Jealous took his gun,
She shot him in the arm.

She never will forgive him,
Though she has other men,
She will take his money,
That's all she wants ye ken.

Ointment for a wounded mind,
When there was but one cure,
Claire heals his mind and salves his wounds,
She's not a witch, I'm sure.

Now Da, is truly happy,
Though he is far away,
I keep him safe inside my heart,
And for his soul I pray.

~

A Lass Comes Riding

So! he's back, don't lie to me!
Seen riding in the Glen,
He is not in the colonies,
Will I get my money then?

Her face was red with anger,
Tears of rage had flowed,
Laoghaire came to Lallybroch,
To claim what she was owed.

A lassie wearing breeches,
Searching for her kin,
Tall and lean with bright red hair,
A Fraser to her skin.

Welcomed by the family,
Brought into the fold,
Jamie has a daughter,
More precious here than gold.

The shrew like voice grew louder,
Wheedled and complained,
Demanded explanation,
Claiming she was shamed!

I'll know who is yer mother?
He did not treat me fair,
It takes a fire to kill a witch,
And she was always there!

I pulled myself to my full height,
My Fraser blood was riled,
I am Jamie Fraser's daughter,
Yes, and I'm Claire's child.

She very near exploded,
She called my mother bitch,
A stream of foul expletives,
Ending up with witch!

Proof was in my pocket,
His mother's wedding gift,
Milk white pearls, a chain of gold.
She mocked them with short shrift.

Hers by right she claimed them,
Claimed she was his wife,
I told them straight, how this foul thing,
Had tried to take Claire's life.

She mumbled on decrying him,
And how he did her wrong,
How he never wanted her,
Claire's love was too strong.

A quiet manic mantra,
Jamie in her arms,
Stolen by the English witch,
Captured by her charms,

Her fetch was in their wedding bed,
He cried for her at night,
She was not dead, a witch must burn
She knew that she was right

A quite voice beside me,
Calming, soft and kind,
Ian Told me Claire was safe,
Like he read my mind.

She found him then! My heart leapt
She wasn't on her own
Reunited with her love,
Through that ring of stone.

They welcome me as one of them,
I'm loved for who I am,
I know they love my father,
He's a good and honest man.

I will travel to them,
far across the sea,
Warn them of a fatal fire.
This is my destiny.

~

Breakfast in a Brothel

A bedroom in a brothel,
And I am not a whore!
A constant stream of visitors
Arriving at the door.

Jamie gone on 'business'
Was I being rude,
To think one of the visitors,
Might be the maid – with food!

I had no clothes to speak of,
The journey ripped my dress,
I wrapped the quilt around me,
No need to impress.

The sound of voices drew me,
Down the flight of stairs,
I know the ladies of the night,
Won't put on any airs!

Food is passed and generously,
The new girl – getting fed,
And sound advice on working,
I feel they are misled.

Dorcas, Peggie, Mollie
Introductions done,
Breakfast in a whorehouse,
Is proving to be fun.

I'm older for a new girl,
But have good skin and tits,
I should do fine, just get some clothes,
A shift that shows my bits!

I must have had a rough one,
The passions of the night,
Are showing red, above the quilt,
My god my man can bite!

They've seen me walking stiffly,
I get some good advice,
If I've been used, and used too hard,
To bathe your bits is nice!

Advice on contraception,
I'm now on firmer ground,
Deep in conversation,
We pass the tips around.

A hearty breakfast eaten,
We chat and face the day,
There's an early customer,
The newbie is first prey!

Top tip for an early one,
To get the business done,
The whole thing happens quicker,
With yer finger up his bum!

Silence! Rolls like tumbleweed,
The girls are all confused
Madame Jeanne has spotted me,
And she is not amused!

The wife of Monsieur Fraser,
Should not breakfast with whores,
Wrapped up in her bedclothes,
Without any drawers!

I bid the girls gracious goodbye,
Leave them to sell their wares,
The sharp French voice of Madame Jeanne
Packs me off upstairs!

~

Into the Wilderness

Bringing it all back

Bonnets gang stole all we had,
We are back again to nought,
My wedding ring I'd swallowed,
How to retrieve it? I'd not thought.

I could feel it stuck there,
A lump, hard in my throat,
Only two ways out of there,
Not pleasant on a boat.

Why does he want the captains pipe?
He seems to have a plan,
Some water, and a bucket,
Aggravating man.

I've seen that look upon his face,
Mischievous intent,
I'm not going to like this much,
I know when he's hell bent!

Tipped into the beaker,
The scrapings from the pipe
Burnt tobacco, ash, and all
He gave its bowl a wipe.

It floated on the water,
The look of it! The stink!
He fixed me with 'obey me' eyes,
And ordered me to drink.

I shook my head, I would not!
The taste would be too vile,
A strong arm reached around me,
He grasped me with a smile.

That Scottish bastard held my nose,
He prised open my mouth,
Then that bloody sadist,
Poured the liquid south!

I heaved and retched; my face turned red
I swallowed then, oh F*@k it!
My stomach contents ring and all
Spewed into the bucket!

I'll have you, Jamie Fraser!
I'm still heaving from that brew,
My insides trying to get out,
And you enjoyed it too!

It's better that way Sassenach
He held his sides with laughter,
If it went through the other way,
Ye'd have tae find it – after!

~

Buckskins

What is that strange garment?
She is nae wearing stays,
I quite like the joggling!
It's a brassiere she says.

To ride into the mountains,
She will'na wear a dress,
Or ride there like a lady,
Aye! she means tae cause me stress.

She's made a pair of breeches,
They cling there is no doubt,
All the world will see her arse,
I can'nae let her out.

I ken that if her mind is fixed,
Reason comes to nought,
She says she's watched my arse for years,
Without impure thought!

Now if I was tae wear the kilt,
She'd ravish me for sure,
She knows just what her whiles will do,
My thoughts are now impure.

I feel her flesh beneath the cloth,
Warm and round and firm,
Shall I remove these buckskin pants?
Then I could make her squirm,

Infuriating Sassenach,
Too well ye know my mind,
I love tae watch ye joggling,
I love yer round behind.

I'll let ye have ye wardrobe,
I have no choice of course,
But the only thing yer sitting on,
'Cept me, will be yer horse!

~

Leaky Roof

It could wait 'til morning,
We could just move the bed,
The icy drip of water landed,
Where he laid his head.

He rose up to investigate,
Searching in the dark,
For signs of water ingress,
Where damp had made a mark,

Tools in hand and ready,
Like a soldier off to war,
Having done reconnaissance,
He's headed for the door,

Hold it soldier, freeze right there,
That's your best wool shirt,
Don't you dare go out to work in that,
You'll ruin it with dirt.

So completely naked
He climbed up on the roof
Expression of a martyr,
As if I needed proof.

Loud dramatic hammering,
A point is neatly made,
Then freezing cold, he climbs back in
The warm bed where I stayed.

Crisis thus averted,
Manly duties done,
The carpenter goes back to sleep,
Cold hands, on my bum.

~

Indecent Exposure

Thrown from my horse, I lay there
In pain that made me groan
No one around to hear me,
I could die out here alone

Lost out in the wilderness,
Unconscious, freezing cold,
Shivering, and muddy,
Exposure taking hold.

Shoes found on the threshold,
Left there by a ghost,
Taken back to safety,
To those I love the most.

Boil the water, Stoke the fire,
Bath before I sleep, serene
I'll not be washing filthy sheets,
If I can sleep there, clean.

Shampoo, soap, hot water,
Whisky for inside,
Muddy clothes abandoned,
Along with female pride.

Tenderly he washed my hair
Cleaned off all the dirt,
Examining my bruises,
Gentle where it hurt.

Aye she's handy with the goose grease
When I have a chill,
'Time, I tested it on her,
I will nae have her ill.

I shall get my own back,
I can'nae let this pass,
Fair is fair - this ointment stinks,
Just like the devil's arse!

The pungent smell of camphor,
Rising from my chest,
It's a thorough application,
Now - He's covering the rest.

Not just for my welfare,
My senses working loose,
The gander's getting saucy
With a very greasy goose.

~

A Disturbance

In my dreams I'd seen her,
And photographs from Claire,
I knew the profile of yer face,
The colour of her hair,

Lost to me across the time,
But safe, in times of peace,
All that will be left of me,
When death brings my release.

I see her always as a bairn
But one I never nursed,
I've nieces and I've nephews,
Seen them grow, my own life cursed.

I've felt her closer lately,
Since we've been at the ridge,
Some sense that she is with me,
Has somehow built a bridge!

No peace for the wicked,
I hear a woman's call,
Can a man not have some peace?
To piss against the wall!

There's something in the tone of voice,
Makes me turn my head,
I am the man she's seeking,
I'll no take her to my bed!

I've coin that I can give her,
If she's needin' food,
But no, she is insistent,
Without being rude.

You are Jamie Fraser?
I am, and I'm confused,
She's tall, her eyes are darkest blue,
Like sky with thunder bruised,

Long red hair, hangs down her back,
My senses start to quiver,
I'm looking in the mirror,
The dawning makes me shiver,

It's Brianna, it's my daughter,
I cannot see my way for tears,
The child I thought was lost to me,
For 200 years.

~

Murtagh – ye old Coot

The Scots are canny with their coin,
We've heard it much in verse,
A tired man, a long day's work,
I'm closed – we hear him curse!

The forge was killed, His hammer quiet,
His tools were on the bar,
A wee Scots voice implored him,
We have tae travel far!

A swift negotiation,
a master robs a boy,
A purse of coin to mend a bit,
From this there'd be no joy.

Dander up, and angry,
He finds the blacksmith in!
Set to get some money back,
No man will fleece his kin

A voice not heard for many years,
The blacksmith turns – so slow,
All those extra shillings,
Were fate, I think we know.

Four eyes filled with tears of joy,
Murtagh has been found,
The tight old coot has found his kin,
Now he must buy a round!

Fifteen extra shillings,
Was little price to pay,
Augousti, I have missed ye so,
Will ye not come to stay.

Cut from Ellen's candlestick
A silver ring is made,
Forged with love and Latin,
His final purchase made!

Beers drunk with Murtagh,
Through time they build a bridge,
Returning home, he will find Claire
And chaos on the ridge!!

Not your Fault

Did you kill Jack Randall?
The question left my lips,
I saw him flinch at just the name,
His hands upon his hips,

The scar that marked inside his thigh,
A gruesome souvenir,
He told me of Culloden,
Did I really want to hear?

He did not remember
who had he killed or how?
But Jack Randall's bloody corpse
Lay on top of him somehow.

Did it make it better?
The fact that he was dead,
Did it silence for all time?
The turmoil in his head?

I told her that in time it fades,
The pain gets less each day,
Now it does not matter,
But it has nae gone away.

She believes it all her fault,
Was there more she could have done?
The rapist who got her with child,
Could she have fought and won?

My words do not convince her
My next, would hurt me more,
I did my best tae anger her
I called my daughter whore!

She slapped me hard,
I fought her, I fought her as a man,
With ease of strength of muscle,
I worked her through my plan.

I showed her how, despite her grit
And her will to win,
She would be overpowered,
At first, she won't give in.

She kicks and bites and struggles,
It cuts me to the bone,
To hear my daughter pleading,
Da! Please stop! I'm done.

Ye could not fight him daughter,
He'd have killed you if ye'd tried,
Don't blame yourself forever,
Time will heal the hurt inside.

Then I walked in darkness,
Prayed my demons gone
Forgave again Jack Randall
For all that he had done.

The Lord says vengeance is all his,
His sentiment is fine,
Sorry Lord, but in this case,
Bree's vengeance will be mine!

~

Breathe Again!

Breathe!
There's rope around my neck,
Breathe!
I am not dead.
Breathe!
A barrel at my feet
A sack over my head.

Breathe!
They did not tie my hands,
One protects my throat
Breathe!
Please see the flag of truce
Hanging from my coat.

Breathe!
I'm hanging, kicking air
But I'm still alive,
Breathe!
Pray God they look for me,
Then maybe I'll survive.

Breathe!

I see them through the sack,
My hold on life is weak,
Breathe!
Thank God, they've seen me,
I can no longer speak.

Breathe!
Strong arms support my weight
The rope no longer tight
Breathe!
I hit the blessed earth
Have I the will to fight?

Breathe again!
I am not dead,
But I am scarce alive,
Claire can give me life again
Pray God I will survive

Breathe!
The last thing that I saw
Hanging from the tree,
When the rope jerked round my neck,
The face I saw was Bree!

Breathe!
I have survived the hanging tree,
My fate was Gods own choice,
He let me keep the ones I love,
But took away my voice.

Breathe!

~

Fever

A child as young a Jemmy,
A father wracked with grief
I fell amongst the mourners,
Like an autumn leaf,

Exhausted, weak, failing,
Fever boiled across my brain,
With sparks of white- hot lightening,
Harbingers of pain.

My skin was tight and brittle,
flesh had burned away,
Pounding blood rang in my ears,
My body baked like clay,

Throat is tight, I cannot breathe,
I cannot take in air,
Faces, voices come and go,
But do not stop and stare,

I reached up and I touched it,
The beam above my head,
My fevered mind reminds me,
It's eight feet above the bed.

I hear voices calling
I must obey them all
Golden eyes the same as mine,
Implore me heed the call.

Braced against the window,
His face lit by the dawn,
Tears of grief run down his face,
A man prepared to mourn,

I only know I love him,
But I don't recall his name,
The amber voice still draws me in,
Will she win the game?

A figure stands beside him,
Her actions draw my eye,
That touch spurs my decision,
I'm not prepared to die

Rough Justice

Malva was already dead,
I tried to save the child,
Denigrated as a witch,
The Browns would hold a trial.

This is revenge, not justice,
Tis all about his brother,
That and petty jealousy,
Mob justice has no honour.

Under guise of safety,
No reason and no law,
No evidence presented,
They'd lynch us that's for sure.

And so, begins a journey,
Helpless at their hands,
Victims of the Christie's
But not one understands,

Easy to condemn a man,
His honour to impugn
Easy to shout 'burn the witch'
My work forgotten soon.

At least we go together,
Two of us, are strong.
What is this, Tom Christie?
Is it for justice you're along?

A deep one is Tom Christie,
He knows I'm not a witch,
There is method in his madness,
On a rope we shall not twitch!

~

Chaos in the Kitchen

Cookie batter in the bowl,
Jemmy waved the spoon,
Grandma can I lick the bowl?
Can I do it soon?

Batter all around his face,
Cookies in to bake,
Jem announces he has lice,
That was the first mistake,

Brianna's search for crawlers,
Lice, in Jemmy's hair,
The smell of burning treacle,
Drifting through the air,

Pulled swiftly from the oven,
Cookies fly across the room,
Adso on the hunt for them,
Stalking in the gloom!

Jamie's burnt his finger,
His pain announced in Gallic,
Holding up a finger,
In a gesture which is phallic.

Chaos in my kitchen,
Go Adso! catch some mice,
We are about to shave some heads,
The men and boys have lice!

~

Life Through a Lens

Sitting in my surgery,
I marvelled at the sight
Held captive now for science,
They swam with all their might.

Deposited the night before,
Evidence of passion,
I'd kept them just to test the lens,
But I'd tease him in my fashion.

What are ye doing Sassenach
He strolled into the room,
Invited then to have a look,
He peered into the gloom.

Are they no gerrrms he queried,
Should they no, have teeth,
I smiled and told him what they were,
Laughing underneath.

They are sperms – male seed.
In confusion then he wallowed,
How on earth did ye come by them?
Eyebrow raised, he swallowed!

You left them with me just last night,
I told him with a wink,
He put his eye back to the lens,
With a two eyed blink.

Look at the wee strivers,
They've handsome tails I see
Quite proud of his effort
He talked of them with glee.

In the right environment
They'll live a week or so.
What ye do then Sassenach,
When ye let them go.

Fine wee things, the seed of life,
I think I've more to send,
When ye've finished watching them
Give them a fitting end!

Lessons in the snow

The traits of male anatomy
Are designed for having fun,
Ye can do things that a lass can't do,
I'll show ye – this is one.

Jemmy and his Grand da
Outside in the snow,
The privy – na we'll not get there,
It is too far ye know,

They came in stamping off the cold,
Warming by the flames
Conspiring in that way of theirs,
Grand da teaching him new games.

Come and look outside he nagged,
I've learned to write my name,
So that's what Grand da's teaching him.
He's getting all the blame.

Well now! No one listens anyway,
To what I ask them to,
And I've only taught him something,
That a lassie can'nae do!

~

Kiss them better

To save us doing laundry,
He stripped off to the waist,
Muscled hard from working,
My request was so misplaced.

I'd seen Da's back few times before,
His shrug says 'din'nae fash'
Years have passed but still they bring,
A memory of the lash.

We strained to move that boulder,
The children helped us NOT!
Dirty, muddy, happy,
We reached the swimming spot.

The mud fight was quite brutal,
They're clay from head to toe,
Every nook and cranny,
Filled with muck ye know.

How do they get so dirty?
Da says there's but one cure,
Dunk them in the swimming hole,
Their screams we must endure!

If ye do not let him try,
ye will nae know he can,
I wait to see if Jem can swim,
Drowning not the plan.

Holding tight to Grand Da,
Legs wrapped around his waist,
Jemmy rode home piggy-back,
He saw what Grand Da faced

Walking home he told them,
Why his back was scarred,
The boys would fight the world for him,
They told him – no holds barred

Then Jemmy kissed that broken skin,
I heard my father wince,
Then he laughed and stretched a bit,
Recovered like a Prince,

Still a reminder of the past
A trigger in his mind
It's why he keeps his shirt on
How could I be so blind

Still taken back into a time,
Of whip, and chain and fetter,
A child's voice behind his ear says
'Jemmy make it better'

~

Aqua Vitae

Germinated barley,
Dried on the floor so well
The malt placed in the mash tub,
Spring water weaves a spell,

Fermented to a liquor
New and harsh to taste,
Matured then within the casks,
Not a drop will waste.

Some sold to keep us solvent,
Some gifted. keeps us free,
Some is aged in ancient caves,
The best I keep for me!

The art of making Whisky,
Goes where we Scots shall roam.
It is Magic sent across the world,
Its taste will take you home.

There are other spirits,
But none of them can beat,
That rolling taste upon yer tongue,
That smell of highland peat.

The flavours of the running burn,
With just a hint of heather,
Strength of granite in its kick,
All made by Highland weather,

Universal coinage,
Produced with love and care,
Raw spirit aged in casks of oak,
Obtains a flavour rare,

More cherished then, than rubies,
More valuable than gold,
Like you and I my Sassenach
Matured as we've grown old.

~

Lizzies Marriage

Freezing cold, we made the trip,
Barrels to the stash
Came the sound of sobbing,
In the bushes near the cache.

A wilted, drunken figure,
There, sat Joseph Wemyss,
Drunk on young raw spirit,
In the ruin of his dreams,

Slung on Jamie's shoulder,
Like the carcass of a deer,
To be warmed up by the fire,
The truth we got to hear.

His daughter Lizzie is with child,
The father isn't known,
Well! she knows it's one of two,
The Beardsley twins! We groan.

Jamie's spitting feathers,
Both of them Ifrinn!!
Gaelic muttered furious,
He calls both brothers in.

Himself intends to 'speak a word'
The matter will be sorted,
Lizzie will be married,
Before she has been courted,

She cannot name the father,
Says she loves them both,
Refuses to take one of them,
Himself lets out an oath!

So, they drew straws for her honour,
Kezzie, has a wife,
Jo must make himself a ghost,
Until there is new life.

Handfast before witnesses,
And before long a priest,
The wean will have parents,
He's seen to that at least.

What goes on between them,
Of that he'll was his hands,
Two lads in just one body,
Is what, Lizzie understands!

~

The Hayloft.

Do ye remember Sassenach,
When we were first together,
Finding places we could hide,
And lie upon the heather,

Like naughty bairns who skipped off school.
We'd rush time through our chores,
Ye'd meet me in the stables,
With the deep straw of the floors,

I could nae wait tae touch ye,
Live flame in my hand,
You burned a path into my heart,
A love that was not planned.

That feeling we could not explain,
Is still as strong for me,
I can'nae lie beside ye,
And not hold ye close ye see.

Yes, I feel the pull of you,
I never need to roam
Wherever this world takes us,
Your body is my home,

High up on the mountain,
We'd lie beneath the stars,
My hands upon your body,
I'd trace your many scars,

Familiar as a route map,
I know each silver line,
Each blade, each burn, each musket ball,
Each stitch which healed was mine,

The match which lit my inner fire,
Was kindled from your flame,
You awoke my inner self,
A thing you still can't tame,

Yes, you are my master,
For as long as I allow,
As I am yours, if you agree,
We both know the score by now,

Fetch a blanket Sassenach,
Let's find a place that's soft,
I recall we used to love,
The hay up in the loft.

Pull up the ladder from the world,
With the horses down below,
I'd make ye scream beneath me,
Dear Lord! I want ye so!

If I can get ye up there,
I shall keep ye there the night,
I'll serve ye well and make ye squeak,
We'll stay there till it's light,

Do you think we have it in us?
We might give the horse a fright,
Remember you're a grandad
Are you up for twice a night?

We lie here in the darkness,
Each other's only thought,
A love as strong as folded steel,
On time's anvil wrought.

I hear Brianna call us,
Our laughter seems most fitting
Tonight, she has no earthly chance,
Of Grand Da babysitting

~

Warriors Prayer

Water fresh straight from the earth,
Wash the world away,
A Warrior, I should cleanse my soul,
Before I face this day,

Make peace with those who went before,
Clear my mind of troubles,
Sluice the guilt of other wars,
Absorb the springs clear bubbles.

Pray to those who in my past,
Have asked no recompense,
Those ones that build my inner wall,
My last line of defence,

I call them down, each one by one,
Pray they bring their shields,
I feel them standing with me,
Their strength says do not yield.

Father, Brother, And my right,
Spirits from my past,
And he who taught me all he knew,
Best I call him last.

Fierce and warlike Uncle,
Ye taught me how tae fight,
No quarter to be given,
Ye never saw that light.

Drawing blood will bring him near,
His lessons call to mind,
Select my enemy with care,
Or cut those ties that bind.

There is no other spirit,
I'd have at my left side,
Fight with me now, in this new fight,
Let justice be yer bride.

Ready now to face what comes,
Kiss me Sassenach,
'Take care Soldier' sends me off,
But your love brings me back.

Resignation

My wife was lying on the ground,
A lead ball in her side,
I saw her fall, I heard the shot,
I feared that she had died,

Lee's messenger was babbling,
I'm wanted on the field,
Tell General Lee to go tae hell,
On this I will na yield,

Claire is lying, ashen,
Her face a mask of pain.
I din nae care what orders come,
I'll not leave her again.

To hell with talk of cowardice,
Desertion, yes and treason.
I've been a traitor all my life,
Is my wife no a good reason?

I tell the lad take off his shirt,
I see the whiteness of his back,
My wife's blood puddled on the floor,
I can make use of that.

I write my resignation,
On skin, with blood for ink.
And send my final message back
Before I've time tae think,

I'm done with all the fighting,
General Fraser is no more,
Ye left my wife tae work outside,
In the middle of a war.

And if Lee sends another,
If it doesn't go as planned,
Tell General Lee to fetch his gun,
He'll shoot me where I stand.

~

A Fraser House

It seems so right we should return
The house knew we would come
It's boarded door and missing panes,
Still bid us call them home.

Empty now for many years,
It wept for occupation,
Its walls had kept a family safe
Until the wars cessation.

Through the generations,
As folk have left the land,
The family home and history,
Passed down hand to hand.

How many ancient Frasers
Still walk within these halls.
Murray's and Mackenzie's too,
Have died inside these walls.

Here's the piece of panel,
The hole is not repaired,
Put there when British searched
But never found the Laird.

There's Da's desk, the huge one,
Where he did all his writing,
His speak a word is left unchanged,
Cosy and inviting.

I feel their presence all around,
Exploring every room,
Imagining my father,
In the priest-hole, in the gloom.

Perhaps they will return here,
Will they feel it strange?
If 200 years apart,
A room is rearranged.

Sometimes when the fires are lit,
When all are gathered round,
I can hear the old house talking,
If we do not make a sound.

It saw the start of many lives,
The ending of a few,
Happy times and tragedy,
It saw some hard times too.

We may well find some secrets,
In the things folk left behind,
But we will never know the tales,
The house keeps in its mind.

It will keep its poker face,
It will guard us with its walls,
It will never let us down,
Broch Tuarach will not fall.

We will keep its history,
Make sure we heed its calls
This Fraser house, has Fraser blood,
Once more inside its walls.

~

Michael Mouse

Who is this, Walter Disney?
Where is this strange place?
Where children learn of fairy tales,
He Disney show his face!

Don't they have their chores tae do?
Or learn to use a knife!
How have they time to waste on things,
On leisure in this life!

I've been told this land is happy,
children love to go,
And play there with the characters,
A giant puppet show.

They should play in the mountains,
Run upon the hills,
Climbing trees and hunting things,
Learn practical skills,

What are moving pictures?
What is a theme park?
What is this fascination?
For sitting in the dark.

I've been told of technology,
Man will fly to the moon,
I'm not sure that I understand,
The need to go so soon!

My grandson is a canny lad,
He lives across the years,
But when he travels through the stones,
It vexes him tae tears.

He must be brave, like Grand Da,
When he leaves our house,
And if he gets to see him,
Give my best tae Michael Mouse!

~

Today's Time Travel

This rock we live on, turns in space,
The third one from the sun.
Revolving on its axis,
It's journey never done.

Divided into many zones,
So, we can all agree
That day is day and night, is night
Time changes, time is free.

A poem written here in Wales,
Will reach you in a blink
It's journey across oceans,
Needs no parchment and no ink.

It flies across the timelines
It's written in my morning,
You may read it in another time,
When your day is dawning

No need for fiery sacrifice,
No need for standing stones
No need to hold a precious jewel
It travels through the zones.

Some go forward, some go back,
Some stay by my side,
Time travelling in the modern world,
The internet their guide.

~

Just Dreaming

Daydreaming

Secret guilty pleasure,
Inhabiting my dreams,
Eyebrow raised in question,
All is not quite how it seems,

Scottish burr as smooth as silk,
Melting down my back,
Raising hairs upon my neck,
Making me lose track,

Candid stare, sees through my soul,
Cerulean eyes,
Colour of the deepest sea,
And never-ending skies,

Your smile, conveys a private thought
No matter who can see,
The message hid behind the smile,
Is meant only for me.

You leap out from the pages,
A literary force,
Invite me on your journey,
Two up on your horse.

I'm really getting comfy,
Wedged between your thighs,
That very sexy Scottish noise
Mixing with my sighs.

I'm jolted back to present day,
My thoughts become obscene,
It doesn't pay to daydream
When the traffic lights turn green!

~

Indecent thoughts

The smell, of sweat, the smell of horse
The subtle scent of leather,
Laid out like a banquet,
Naked in the heather,

Red hair glowing in the sun,
Copper lights on fire,
Half a smile seducing me,
An object of desire.

Never ending muscled limbs,
Tinged with flecks of gold,
Lie upon a tartan plaid,
Never growing old.

Protection from your body,
The last thing on my mind,
Hold me fast and do your worst,
A vixen you may find.

Warrior's hands upon my skin,
Weave a spell of lust,
I'm losing sense of place and time,
I'm crumbling to dust,

Soft lips upon my body,
Know their work so well,
Hidden teeth, nip playfully,
Tongue completes the spell.

My mind vacates my body,
I hear myself cry out,
Bound as one, in heart and mind,
One body without doubt.

In the pages of my book,
My fantasy exists,
This Jamie Fraser is all mine,
Through times eternal mists.

~

A bit of Welsh Passion

Resurrect the romance,
I thought I'd have a go,
Things were getting a bit stale,
In the bedroom don't ya know!

I think I'll change the décor,
Make it nice and cosy,
Some throws and rugs around the place,
A fire would make things rosy.

Heaps of fur upon the bed,
Candles all around,
But I can't find that man of mine,
He's really gone to ground.

I think he's watching rugby,
Or gone out with the boys,
Or maybe in his man cave
Playing with his toys.

A voice is calling from my book,
Right beside my bed,
I turn a page and instantly,
An image in my head,

The pages all fall open,
As if I'm in a dream,
I'm of to Scotland in my mind,
To re-enact THAT scene.

Hark, I hear him coming home,
He weaves his way upstairs,
Crashes through the bedroom door,
Falls into the chairs.

I think he's in another scene,
The romance is all stripped
He's where the Laird got very drunk
This wasn't in my script.

He's really very sorry,
My rugby watching hunk,
He's mine and I forgive him,
But he's really very drunk.

167

He crashes out across the bed,
Laughing to himself,
An elephant has landed,
My book falls off the shelf.

Dream disturbed, romance gone,
Men are such hard work,
My inner Claire Is surfacing,
Where did I put that dirk!

~

The Poet Comes Home

I'm sitting in my favourite spot,
Flicking through the pages,
Looking for a passage,
I haven't read in ages.

I scratch my head, I think of words,
I have another look,
Is it my imagination,
Or is it really in the book.

My mind is looking out to sea
The view goes on forever,
I conjure words inside my mind,
Compose my next endeavour.

Sunshine warm upon my back,
I'm face down in the clover
I watch the busy bees hum by,
My need for words is over.

I hear the humming of the stones,
The awful sounds they make,
Calling for my wandering soul,
A leap of faith to take.

Where will I land, when is the time,
Who is it calls me through,
Someone on the other side,
Someone whose heart is true.

Time is folding back the years,
The arms that catch me strong,
I'm wrapped in plaid and carried home,
But something feels quite wrong.

A voice is calling from afar,
A familiar voice to me!
Put down your book, the suns gone down,
Come in and have your tea!

He's wrapped me in a blanket,
And left me there to sleep,
In my garden full of dreams,
On this hillside steep.

We all dream of a Jamie,
Written in a book,
Perhaps you've really got one
If you'd only look.

Someone who does the small stuff,
Who wipes away your frown,
Who loves you in your darkest hours?
When your sun goes down

~

The Waterfall

Springtime finds me wandering,
High up in the fields,
The sun that warms my winter bones,
Removes my homespun shields.

My body longs for freshness,
Relief from winters grime,
A shower in the waterfall.
Wouldn't be a crime.

The men are working in the fields,
There's little here to see
Naked in the deluge,
There's no one here but me

Water cascades through my hair,
Its silver coats my skin,
A season's cares are washed away,
New life is washing in!

Movement in the bushes,
Says I'm not alone,
A six-foot red-haired water sprite,
Sits naked on a stone,

Beckons me come hither,
Eyes lock on to mine,
Drawing me into his arms,
Is he here by design?

Sassenach, I followed you,
I knew ye'd take a dip,
I've been waiting for this weather,
Just to watch you strip.

I mean to make ye beg me,
I need to use ye so.
I haven't seen ye naked since
The falling of the snow.

Engulfed in falling water,
Encased within his arms,
Hard up against the rocky wall,
He's using all his charms,

They say that great minds think alike,
And spring the mating season,
The man can read me like a book.
He does not need a reason.

His mouth on mine, my master,
I'm plunged into the dark,
My book has fallen on my face,
I'm lying in the park.

Concern is all around me
They think I cry in pain,
I'm red faced with embarrassment
Outlander I explain!

~

The Joys of Technology

Technology is marvellous,
If I'm travelling far.
I can listen to my audiobook,
Through the speakers in my car.

Fellow drivers think I'm mad,
I'm filling up with tears,
Claire just went back through the stones,
To Frank and all her fears.

Jamie's lying on the field,
He's grey and nearly dead,
But he can feel the soul of Claire,
And see her in his head.

It's really quite relaxing,
I can even use my voice,
Ask it to play chapters,
An endless realm of choice.

I can adjust the volume,
I've speakers all around,
You can tell I'm at Culloden,
By the shaking of the ground.

The only little drawback,
Which tends to make one blush,
Is ordering a drive through,
When I'm in a rush.

If I use the order phone
The frequency does match.
McDonald's get Claire's squeaky noise,
Blasting through the hatch.

I fumble with the volume,
In my haste you call them back,
And then they hear that Scottish voice,
Growling Sassenach!

I drive off in a hurry,
Embarrassed for the day,
And now I'm wanted by the cops,
Guess who forgot to pay!

The Great Escape

The walls were bare, the bed was hard,
The blanket made me itch,
I stared up at the ceiling
Thinking life could be a bitch.

They'd taken all my stuff away,
Twas in a plastic bag,
Yes, the coppers had caught up with me,
Like many an old lag.

I'm waiting for the morning,
When I get my day in Court,
To explain away a Happy Meal
Which I really thought I'd bought.

I'm hearing a commotion,
The fire alarm it wails,
Then all the cell doors open,
A modern thing for Wales,

The throbbing of an engine,
A Harleys growl I hear,
My hero revving up his hog
It's music to my ear,

He brought Murtagh and Rupert,
And wee Angus just for sport,
To teach the Cops a lesson,
An interesting thought.

The clash of swords, and musket fire,
They fight outside the door,
Tulach Ard, I hear him yell,
They'll get me out for sure.

Like Jacobite Hells Angels
With me perched upon the back,
Wrap yer arms around my waist,
And hold on Sassenach!

Heading north to Scotland,
If I ever made a million,
I'd give it all, and then some more,
To be sat upon his pillion.

Arms wrapped tight around his waist,
Face buried in his leather,
I breathe in the scent of man,
And petrol, yes and heather,

The bells are my alarm clock
I'm not punished for my sins
The noises were the garbage men
Emptying the bins!

That throaty revving engine,
I think I'll take a pass,
It's just my next-door neighbour,
Outside cutting grass.

My hero wasn't Jamie,
And for certain wasn't Sam,
It's my husband with my coffee,
Is it too early for a dram!

~

Working Out

Like a lot of ladies,
I do frequent the gym,
I like to keep myself in shape,
In case I might meet HIM.

But I have reached a time of life,
When it doesn't do much good,
Pounding out the treadmill miles,
Does not do what it should.

I push some weights,
I go quite red, Ladies only glow!
I suspect I'm not a lady,
I sweat a lot you know.

I spend hours listening,
Watch the flora and the fauna,
Clocking up the mileage,
On the Watt bike in the corner,

Sitting on the saddle,
I've really, quite a view,
An arse that is so awesome
It can crack walnuts in two.

His hair is slightly ginger,
Shoulders very broad,
Heavy stubble nicely trimmed,
He stops me feeling bored.

Six feet three with endless legs,
And muscles on his arms,
He's right there on the cross trainer,
Exhibiting his charms,

I see him in the mirror,
And this confirms my fear,
He really only looks like our-
Sam Heughan from the rear.

Imagine my embarrassment,
Before I've time to think,
'Big Chris' from the Midlands,
Greets me – with a wink!

Heat Wave

It's hot! Too hot for horses,
It's hot! Too hot for dogs,
Too hot to do much work outside,
Too hot for chopping logs,

I have a plan, I shall sneak off,
Quietly, book in hand.
Stolen hours of peace and quiet,
In another land.

I think I'll go and find a tree,
And lie down in its shade,
And dream of Jamie Fraser,
In some leafy glade,

Dappled light falls on a plaid,
Catlike, silent through the trees,
Blue eyes searching for me,
Enjoying what he sees.

Quiet conversation,
Bannocks, cheese and beer,
Relaxing in the sunshine,
No one will find us here.

Safe until the sun goes down,
My book upon my face,
Me and Jamie Fraser,
Lost in time and space.

~

Tequila Dreams

Summer nights in far off lands,
Days in darkened bars,
Lying breathless in the sand
Underneath the stars,

Galloping along the tide,
Riding in the waves,
Dusty days in fields of blue,
Working hard as slaves,

Cold Beer chilling off your thirst,
Friendships formed and more,
Comrades of the closest kind,
Who have your back for sure!

Drink to comrades old and new,
Drink to those we've lost,
Drink to those who stand by you
And never count the cost.

Line the glasses on the bar,
We will forget them not.
Tequila neat, is in the air
When the barman calls the shots,

Liquid gold, a fiery trail,
Burning down my throat,
He takes me gently in his arms,
Tells me get my coat,

Lips are soft upon my mouth,
Hands upon my waist,
Entices me to go with him,
An offer made in haste,

Do I dare to cross the line?
How would we recover?
Would this friendship now be lost?
If I become his lover?

My legs are weak, My stomach leaps,
My senses tell me go,
His body is in tune with mine,
My brain is yelling no!

This man that I have wanted so,
Is laid out on a plate,
I know that I must tell him no
Before it is too late.

I've known him for so very long,
I see into his soul,
I would not lose his friendship,
That could never be my goal.

We could taste forbidden fruit,
A need that must be fed
Or is it curiosity,
Has raised its ugly head

We stagger, laughing at ourselves,
Looking at the stars,
His eyes tell mine he knows the score,
He will not step too far,

We lie together on the sand,
We talk on endless themes,
My best friend for the rest of time,
Locked in Tequila Dreams

Dust Clouds

Dust clouds rise from, horses' hooves,
Haze shimmers from the ground,
Sun beats down from azure skies,
No welcome shade is found,

Twitching ears hear soft spoke words,
Both longing to be free
The long walk home when work is done,
Two in harmony,

Cooling water bathes her skin,
Runs softly down her back,
Muscles twitch in pleasure,
Relaxing – free of tack,

The gaucho tending to his horse,
Her welfare not delayed
He beats the dust from sun browned skin,
And leaves her in the shade.

Long legs clad in denim,
Topped off by a hat,
Blue eyes shaded from the sun,
He moves lithe as a cat,

Too much social media
Is not good for a lass,
Instagram and Twitter,
Lie with me in the grass,

I dreamed I was in Mexico,
I dreamed I was that horse,
I dreamed there was a gaucho,
It was HIM of course.

The bar was so inviting,
His voice tied me in knots,
The beer was icy cold and crisp,
Then he called the shots!

The sun has hardly left the sky,
I can hardly stand,
There's a bottle of tequila,
Empty in my hand!

RDA Camp 2021

Four days of fun packed chaos,
Camp 2021,
Horses, ponies, kids, and tents,
Can anything go wrong.

Day one, it was sunny,
Not a cloud, over the yard.
Horses brushed and plaited,
Riders working hard.

We rode out on the common,
Laughter filled the air,
Learned a lot of pony parts,
Learned to ride with flair.

On Thursday it was raining,
Boy did we get wet,
Cleaning tack was soggy,
It was the best day yet!

Friday crew show jumping!
And made some use of Tim,
Polished up with Windolene,
There's a lovely shine on him.

Granny is exhausted,
This week has been such fun,
Healthy competition
Rosettes for everyone.

Pixie, Poacher, Arthur,
And Jesse all raise a cheer!
They'd love it if you all came back,
But they're tired until next year.

~

The Scottish Volunteer

My reverie was shattered
My dream was real I'm sure
A horse as black as midnight
Charged across the moor.

A rider armed with sword and Dag!
Dressed in highland gear,
Wild hair flying round his face,
A scream inspiring fear!

Through the gate into the yard,
It ruined coffee break,
A trail of devastation
lying in his wake.

He galloped straight into the school,
Dismounted with panache,
Apologised profusely
I'm late! but din'nae Fash.

He talked of how to use a sword,
Of killing with a dirk,
They watched in rapt amazement
As he made his magic work

He dipped into his sporran
And then produced a flask.
Began to pass the whisky round
Without a thought to ask.

The kids were strangely silent,
The ponies stood quite still,
Our RDA camp mystery guest,
Just didn't fit the bill.

He drew his broadsword from its sheath
It glimmered steely blue,
Fixed me with his azure stare
I knew what I would do,

Are ye watching Sassenach,
He whispered in my ear,
And then he taught the lesson,
My Scottish Volunteer.

They learned the warrior's dismount,
Like fiends they learned to scream,
They learned that they were all one Clan,
Working as a team.

He left as quickly as he came,
The kids all gave a cheer
A cloud of plaid a puff of smoke,
Will he come back next year?

Woken by my husband
A dream again I fear,
Still smelling strong of hay and horse,
Still In my riding gear.

I've been sleeping in the chair
Exhausted by my day
Whisky poured he pulls my boots
From him I'll never stray.

~

Covid Dreams

I've had my first injection,
To fight this COVID thing.
They told me of the side effects,
Said my arm might sting,

I was fine when I got home,
For an hour or two,
Then I began to feel quite ill,
Like I had the flu.

I went to bed but couldn't sleep,
I tossed and turned a lot,
When, finally, I drifted off,
This dream just hit the spot,

We used to own a horse box,
An ancient bit of kit
With a bunk behind the driver's seat,
Where us kids would sit.

I also had a boyfriend
And he was six feet three,
A little like Clint Eastwood,
Well! that's how he looked to me.

Back to the dream, I hear you shout,
I'll tell you it was snowing,
Driving in the lorry,
Don't know where we were going,

We got stuck in a snow drift,
We'd be there for the night,
With one bunk and one blanket,
Now that would be a fight,

Enter to my vivid dream,
One Jamie and one Sam
All wedged inside this tiny cab.
With me and Clint – oh damn.

I remember turning over,
And then I went to sleep,
Wrapped in a horse blanket
Which man would I keep?

That bunk is very narrow,
someone had to go,
So, I dumped my boyfriend,
Outside in the snow.

~

Profanity and Argument

I am not an angel,
and I've worked a lot with men,
A burst of foul language
Pops up now and then,

I have a full vocabulary,
Developed over years,
In fact, I learned some novel words,
Too rude for sailors' ears.

A time and place for everything,
Is what my mother taught,
She'd be spinning in her grave,
If she heard the words I've thought.

Speak as you are spoken to,
To your audience relate,
Politeness is the first defence,
If you wish to denigrate,

If you are not understood,
Then get a point across,
using no four-letter words,
That will have them at a loss

But have the big guns ready,
Prime them well for use,
Aim the with some accuracy,
And stand back for abuse.

~

Misspent youth

When I was a teenager
My brothers called me feral,
I ran away, I stayed out late,
A scruffy, dirty rebel.

I hated school – though I was bright
That was par for the course
I'd skip the bus and spend my day
On the mountain with my horse.

Weekends spent not studying
Schoolwork I was mocking.
Exams just drifted by me.
My results were really shocking.

I signed on at the school of life
I learned all sorts of skills,
I can turn my hand to most things.
As long as I don't get killed.

I drifted through a college course,
I didn't much enjoy,
But the things I learned while doing it
I still at times employ.

And then I fell into the job
Where I spent my life
Juggling it with horses
And being someone's wife.

I am not disappointed
With the path I chose,
I've fallen in life's potholes.
I've climbed out of all of those.

Something must have rubbed off
On the days I went to class
For I can never spend the day
Just sitting on my arse.

So, I picked my pen up
And wrote in basic rhyme
My thoughts up on that mountain
Where I spent most of my time.

And, if you need to find me,
If I'm not around,
I'm on my mountain, book in hand,
But please don't make a sound!

~

Hero's.

Let's take a virtual wander,
Through the mind of man,
The beauty and the cruelty,
Of a short attention span,

Some love creating hero's,
Through them they live their lives,
Moulding and remoulding,
Until not much survives.

If your hero's narrative,
Doesn't fit the frame,
You cut and paste and alter,
And then you change the name.

A plastic, superficial world,
Where human life is cheap,
Where you never scratch the surface,
And beauty is skin deep.

Silence all the critics,
With whom you don't agree,
Retreat into your made- up world,
Your life of fantasy,

Play your games with people's minds,
Break them on your wheel,
Have no thought that hero's
Also eat and sleep and feel

Beware of what the future holds,
In this time of plenty,
Will come a time your hero's break,
And your pedestals are empty.

~

The naughty step

Some people feel a pressing need,
To step on a few toes,
On subjects which impassion them,
I must be one of those,

I need to take a lesson,
Bite down on my lip,
Not rise to bitching and to bait,
Not let composure slip,

Some people have a complete knack,
Of pulling all your strings,
Bringing out your devil,
And all the strife that brings,

Strangers that you've never met,
And never ever will,
Taunt you with their insults,
Then go in for the kill,

I have quite broad shoulders,
I left school long ago,
I am not hurt by playground taunts,
If I, am I'll let you know,

I am on the naughty step,
Moderated for 12 hours,
If I should die in exile,
Please don't send me flowers.

~

Acknowledgements

As always full acknowledgement is given to the fact that the characters used in these poems are created by Diana Gabaldon and are from the Outlander series of books and the TV Series.

My work is a tribute to her brilliance and the popularity of her novels.

Thanks are given to the users of the social media fan pages where these poems are also published, from these pages I have received constructive criticism, advice on spelling, grammar, and content. Some of you have now also become friends outside of cyber space!

Credit to my former colleague Leighton Bennetta for allowing use of his photographs for the cover image.

I would also mention here the staff and volunteers of Bridgend County RDA, South

Wales and Mount Pleasant RDA, South Wales.

And lastly my poster boy Criccieth Pixie

Thank You

Copyright page

Other books by the Author

This book is the seventh book in a series of Unofficial Books of Outlander inspired poetry.

Unofficial Droughtlander Relief.

The Droughtlanders Progress.

Totally Obsessed.

Fireside Stories.

Je Suis Prest.

Apres Le Deluge

I hope the Princess will Approve – a book of COVID and Horse related poems.

....

Ginger like Biscuits - the adventures of a Welsh Mountain Pony.

Email: chestyathome@aol.com

Thank You
For Your Support of
Riding For the Disabled
Best Regards

Maggie J

211

RDA

Riding for the Disabled Association
Incorporating Carriage Driving

It's what you can
do that counts

Made in the USA
Columbia, SC
05 May 2022